Juanita Du Toit

The Curious Chameleon

Bumblebee Books
London

BUMBLEBEE PAPERBACK EDITION

Copyright © Juanita Du Toit 2022

The right of Juanita Du Toit to be identified as author of
this work has been asserted in accordance with sections 77 and 78 of the Copyright, Designs and Patents Act 1988.

A CIP catalogue record for this title is
available from the British Library.

ISBN: 978-1-83934-488-6

Bumblebee Books is an imprint of
Olympia Publishers.

First Published in 2022

Bumblebee Books
Tallis House
2 Tallis Street
London
EC4Y 0AB

Printed in Great Britain

www.olympiapublishers.com

Dedication

I dedicate this book to my person, my husband and best friend, David. Thank you for encouraging me to follow my dreams of becoming an illustrator.

Once upon a time, there was a curious chameleon.
His name was Gerald. Gerald lived in the garden.
He loved eating flies and enjoyed playing hide-and-seek.

On Sunday, Gerald was sitting in a tree, when a girl appeared. Her name was Gigi. She liked to paint in the garden.

Gerald was curious...
so while Gigi was painting, he moved into her basket of flowers.

Gigi heard something moving near her basket and turned around to have a look. She saw the most adorable and colourful little chameleon.

Gigi was so excited to meet a new friend...

that she decided to take him home.

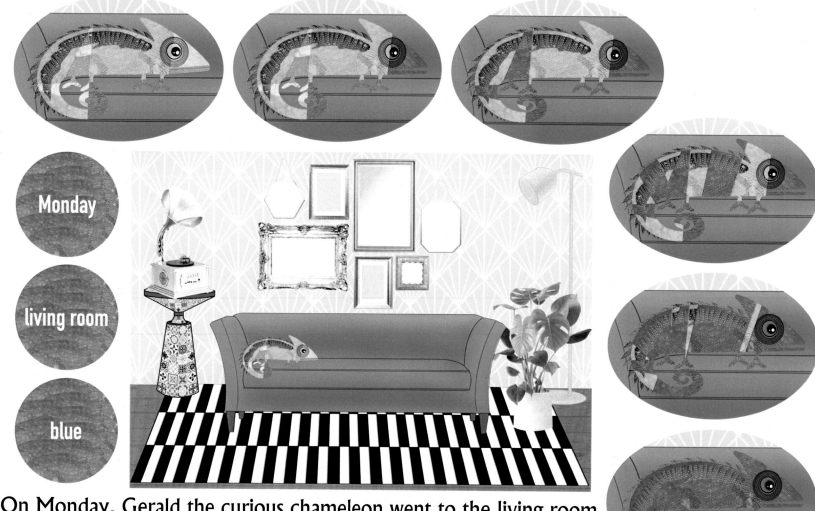

On Monday, Gerald the curious chameleon went to the living room.
He sat on the sofa and turned blue. He ate one fly.

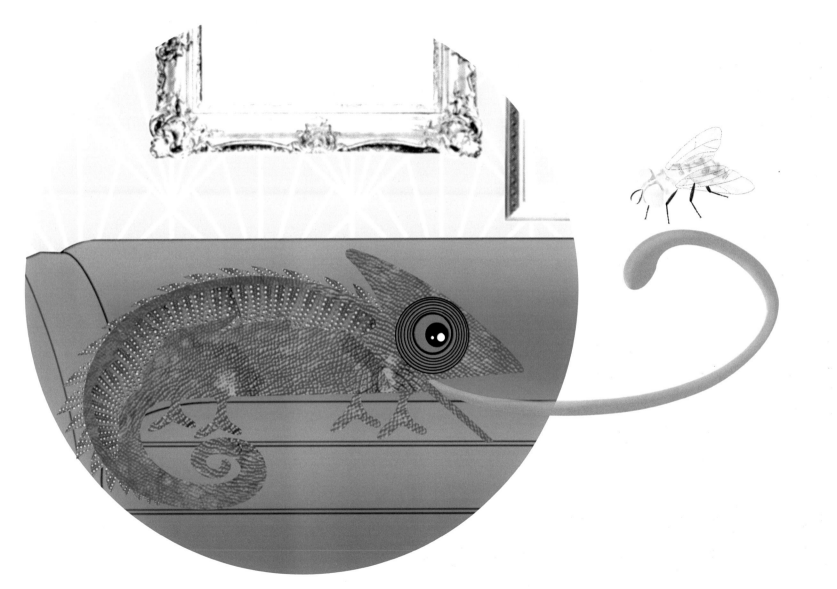

Gigi looked for him in the living room...

but couldn't find him anywhere?

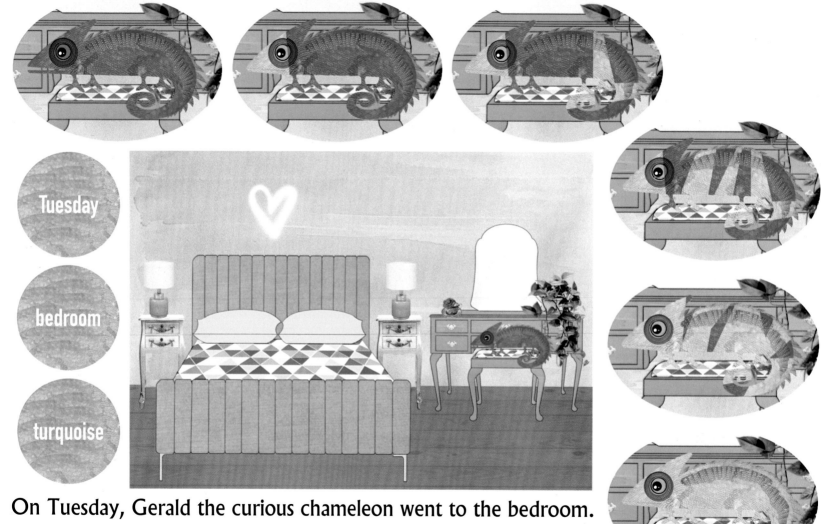

On Tuesday, Gerald the curious chameleon went to the bedroom.
He sat on the stool and turned turquoise. He ate two flies.

Gigi looked for him in the bedroom...

but couldn't find him anywhere?

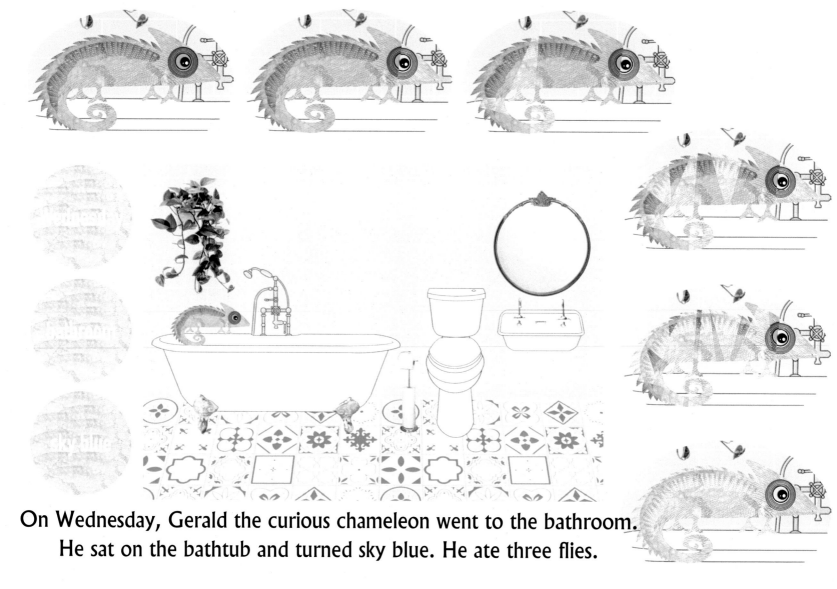

On Wednesday, Gerald the curious chameleon went to the bathroom. He sat on the bathtub and turned sky blue. He ate three flies.

Gigi looked for him in the bathroom...

but couldn't find him anywhere?

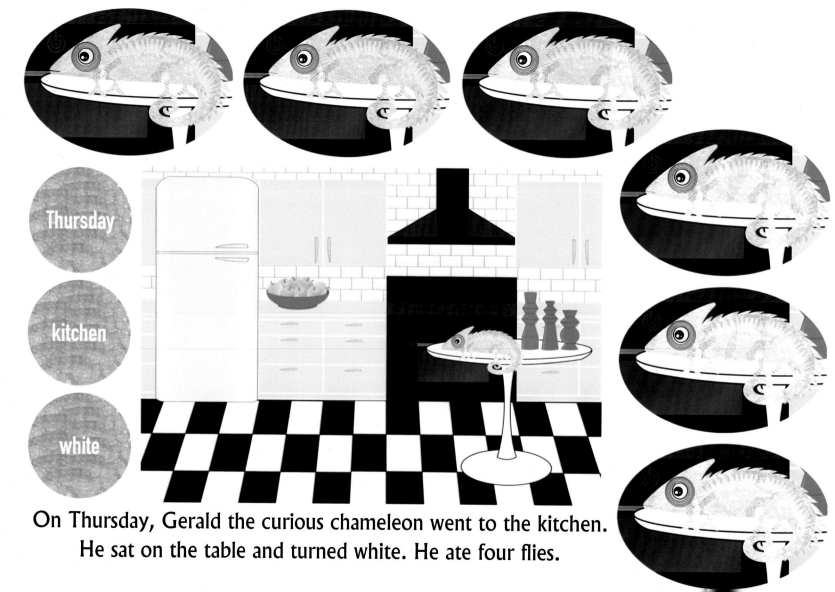

Thursday

kitchen

white

On Thursday, Gerald the curious chameleon went to the kitchen.
He sat on the table and turned white. He ate four flies.

Gigi looked for him in the kitchen...

but couldn't find him anywhere?

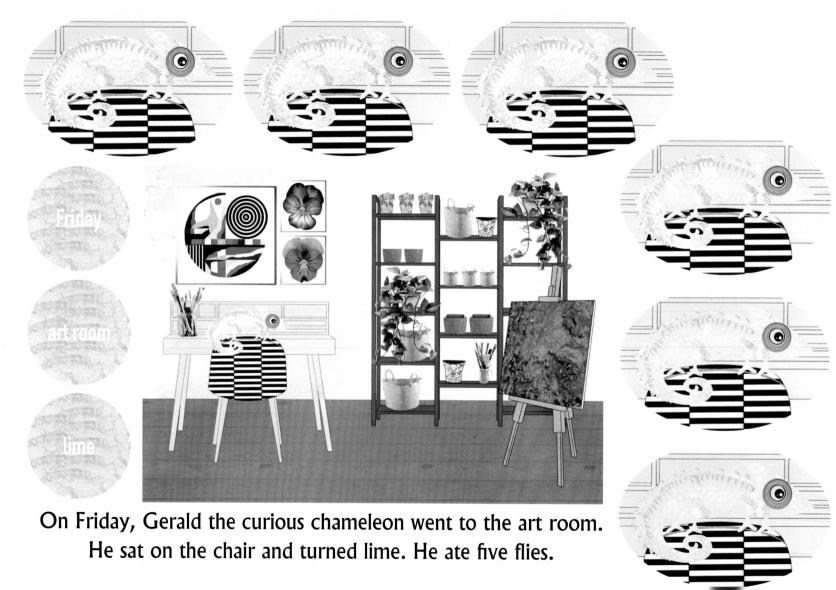

On Friday, Gerald the curious chameleon went to the art room.
He sat on the chair and turned lime. He ate five flies.

Gigi looked for him in the art room...

but couldn't find him anywhere?

On Saturday, Gigi went to the garden.
When she put down her basket, Gigi heard something move inside it.

She was so surprised and excited to see...

the most adorable little...

Chameleon!

After that, Gigi went to visit
Gerald in the garden every day.

About the Author

Juanita grew up in a small picturesque seaside village in South Africa. She has a BEd (Hons) degree and has been teaching abroad for many years. Juanita has always loved drawing and being creative. Growing up, she dreamt of becoming a children's book illustrator one day. With encouragement from her husband, she started studying illustration part-time. Juanita loves the ocean, traveling, wildflowers, puppies and daydreaming.

Acknowledgements

Thank you to my brother, Jan, who sent me a photograph of a little chameleon he met one day. It was the inspiration for this story. Thank you to my mum, for inspiring me with all her imaginative storytelling over the years.